W9-AMV-538

Her Majesty, Aunt Essie

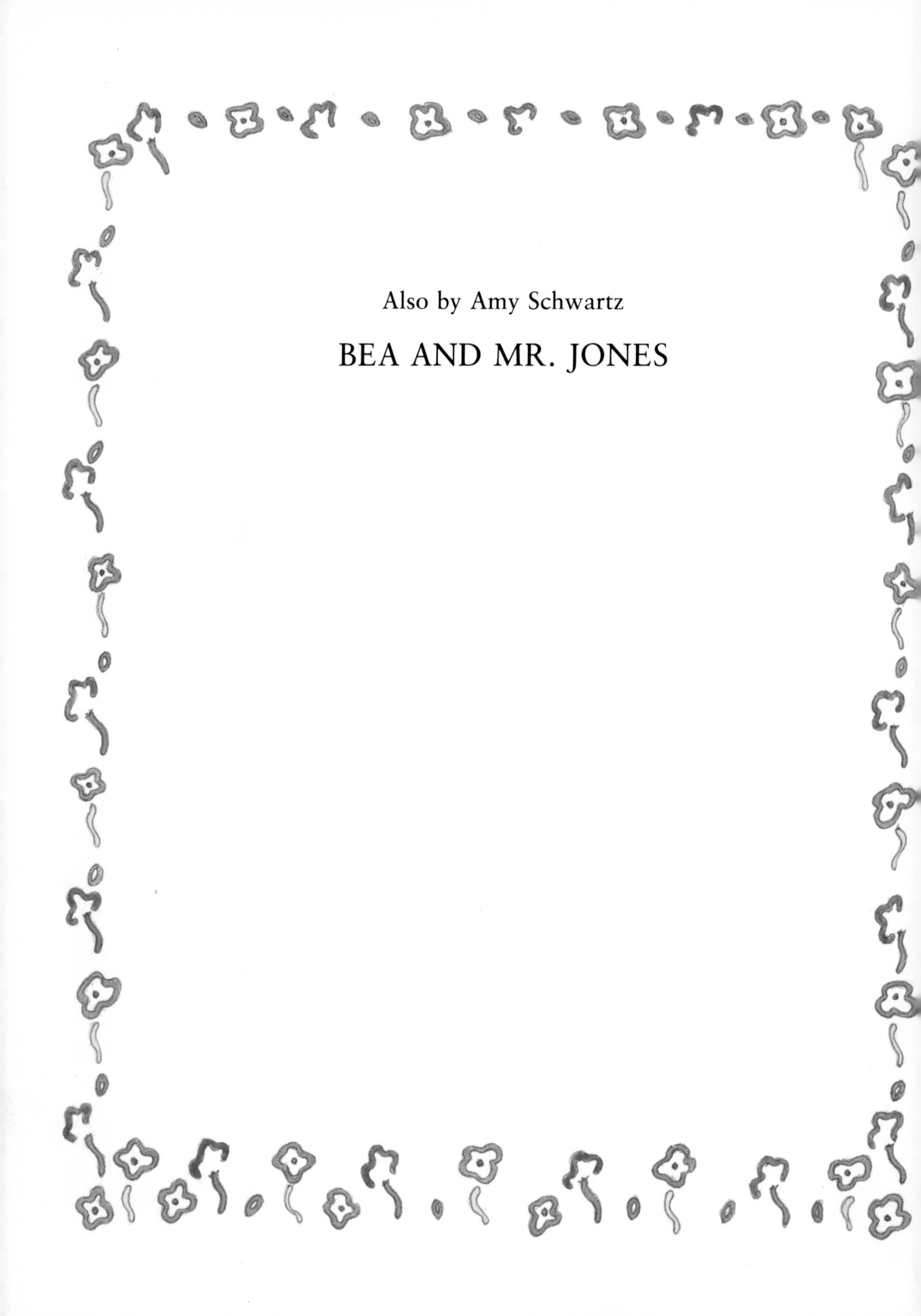

Also by Amy Schwartz

BEA AND MR. JONES

Her Majesty, Aunt Essie

by
Amy Schwartz

BRADBURY PRESS SCARSDALE, NEW YORK

Bradbury Press, Inc.
2 Overhill Road Scarsdale, N.Y. 10583
An Affiliate of Macmillan, Inc.
Collier Macmillan Canada, Inc.
Manufactured in the United States of America
10 9 8 7 6 5 4 3 2 1
The text of this book is set in 16. pt. Sabon. The illustrations are pencil and watercolor wash reproduced in full color.
Library of Congress Cataloging in Publication Data
Schwartz, Amy.
Her Majesty, Aunt Essie.
Summary: Ruthie boasts to her best friend that her aunt is a queen and then has to prove it.
1. Children's stories, American. [. Aunts—Fiction.
2. Friendship—Fiction] I. Title.
PZ7.S406He 1984 [E] 8411003
ISBN 0-02-781450-5

For Julie

My Aunt Essie used to be a Queen.
I knew it the day she moved in.

The first thing Aunt Essie unpacked was a big picture of a man with a moustache and a sash across his chest.

A King if I ever saw one.

And when I helped Aunt Essie put away her jewelry, she let me try on a pair of those long dangling earrings. Only a Queen has earrings like that.

I didn't want to give the earrings back.

Aunt Essie said, "When I was a girl I was a little princess, Ruthie, not like some children I know."

So there. She told me herself.

At dinner Aunt Essie held her little finger out when she drank her tea, just like a Queen.

And you should have seen the way she talked to Daddy when we washed the dishes. I could tell she was used to giving orders.

After we'd cleaned up, Aunt Essie phoned her friend Mrs. Katz and talked for a long time. She kept looking around our apartment and clutching her heart and sighing and saying things in French.

Well, no one else I know acts like that.
Before I went to bed, I drew a family tree.
There I was, right next to Kings and Queens.

In the morning I showed the family tree to Maisie-next-door. Maisie laughed so hard I thought she'd split. I grabbed my drawing back.

"I can prove it!" I said. "I'll prove it by midnight tonight . . . or . . . or you can have my dog Joe!"

Maisie stopped laughing.

"It's a deal," she said.

All morning I stayed close to Aunt Essie, keeping my eyes open.

She talked to the vegetable man just the way a Queen would, but Maisie wasn't with me.

I saw a little gold crown on the hem of Aunt Essie's slip, but how could I show Maisie that?

I asked Maisie over for the afternoon, hoping proof would turn up.

Maisie and I played cards for a while. Then Aunt Essie called from the bath.

"Oh Ruthie, won't you help me scrub my back?"

"Aunt Essie used to have ten ladies in waiting to help her wash," I said to Maisie as we went into the bath.

"Ten ladies in waiting and one butler to turn on the hot water and another one to turn it off."

When Aunt Essie was out of the bath, Mrs. Katz came over for a visit. They sat on the balcony and waved to their friends in the street.

"Just like at her coronation," I said to Maisie.

Aunt Essie's boyfriend Walter drove by and honked the horn in his new convertible.

Mrs. Katz clucked her tongue.
"Like a royal carriage," she said.
I poked Maisie in the ribs.
"Not good enough," Maisie said.
I put Joe in the backyard where Maisie couldn't keep looking at him.

Well, dinnertime came and Maisie still didn't believe me.

After supper I went out and sat on the stoop.
Maisie came out too.

"You only have four hours left," Maisie said.

I felt so low that when Walter showed up
for his date with Aunt Essie and tickled me on the toes
I didn't even laugh.

I was just about to tell Maisie I gave up
and I hoped she'd let me visit Joe when there was a hustle
and bustle at the front door.

We heard Walter say, "Essie! You look more
magnificent than ever!"

Then Aunt Essie sailed out the door.

She was wearing a long satin gown. She had a fur stole over her shoulders. She was wearing those long dangling earrings, and—you can have everything I own, if I'm lying—there was a gold crown on her head.

I jumped up.

"Your majesty," I said. I bowed low. I stayed there.

Maisie sucked in her breath. Then there was silence. I could feel Aunt Essie's eyes on me. More silence. Then I felt a hand on my head.

"Princess Ruth," Aunt Essie said. "You may arise."

Then Walter ran ahead and opened the convertible door. Aunt Essie floated into the car. And they were gone.

Well, I didn't punch Maisie or say "I told you so" or anything.

Those of us with royal blood don't do that sort of thing.

E
Sch
Schwartz, Amy
Her Majesty, Aunt
Essie
DISCARDED
Central School Library
Ithaca, N. Y.
BTSB
Bound to Stay Bound Books, Inc.